Laurel Finds A Friend

Janice Goldacker

Illustrated by Sue Lynn Cotton

Sarasota, Florida

Copyright © Janice Goldacker, 2015

All rights reserved. Published by the Peppertree Press, LLC. the Peppertree Press and associated logos are trademarks of the Peppertree Press, LLC.

No part of this publication may be reproduced, stored in a retrieval system, transmitted in any form or by any means, electronic, mechanical, photocopying, recording, or otherwise, without prior written permission of the publisher and author/illustrator. Graphic design by Rebecca Barbier. Illustrations by Sue Lynn Cotton.

For information regarding permission,
call 941-922-2662 or contact us at our website:
www.peppertreepublishing.com or write to:
the Peppertree Press, LLC.
Attention: Publisher
1269 First Street, Suite 7
Sarasota, Florida 34236

ISBN: 978-1-61493-338-0

Library of Congress Number: 2015901619

Printed February 2015

Laurel is a very pretty and clever squirrel. She lives in a tree house behind Periwinkle Farm; the woods are called Periwinkle Woods. When Laurel woke up this morning she didn't think that she was going to have a special day, just the usual summer morning.

Periwinkle Woods is a beautiful place. In the early morning the sun shines through the trees and sparkles on a little pond in the middle of the woods. It is Laurel's favorite time of day and this morning was especially nice for a walk.

She was ready for breakfast and knew right where she could go and search. She knows a place where the acorns are "The Best" and this time of year she can find nuts and berries.

As Laurel turned the corner at the big rock she heard a small crackling sound. She stopped to listen and the sound became louder and closer. She then heard a small cry and the sound of something falling through the trees.

Just as she looked up something or someone fell right in front of her. It was a small gray squirrel, a girl squirrel and the second after she hit the ground she was on her feet.

"Hi, my name is Millicent, what's yours?" the little squirrel asked.

"I am Laurel. Are you all right?"

"Yes, I am fine, I'm an acrobat and I was practicing my routine."

Not wanting to be rude Laurel said, "Oh, I am really glad that you are not hurt." She really wanted to ask if Millicent's routine was always to fall through the trees, but didn't want to hurt her feelings.

Laurel and Millicent had a wonderful morning, sharing stories and becoming friends. Laurel told Millicent of her flower garden and taking dance lessons from the old squirrel, Miss Dominique.

Millicent talked of her adventures in the Emerald Meadow, crossing the big, very scary road and how she taught herself to be an acrobat.

Later, they had lunch and laid in the meadow and watched the clouds drift by; they laughed about the shapes of the clouds and what they resembled. "That one looks like an ice cream cone!" Millicent said.

"Sure does," Laurel replied, "and that one looks like a bird flying."

Millicent laughed, "Silly, that is a bird!" They both laughed until they were crying.

In the corner of her eye Laurel saw Danny trying to sneak up on the two of them. He was creeping through the bushes as quietly as a mouse. Danny is a friend of Laurel's and he is always up to something. She knew he wanted to surprise them and make them shriek with fright.

She whispered to Millicent "Someone is sneaking up on us, when I say 'go' turn around and say "BOO!!!"

When Danny was just a few feet away from them, Laurel said "GO!" and they both made one quick turn and shouted in their best outdoor voice "BOO!!!" Danny rolled up in a ball and did two back summersaults; he ended up on his back with his feet sticking up in the air.

"That was a mean trick" said Danny, while trying to catch his breath.

Laurel said, "No, you were going to scare us, we just caught you first."

Millicent was laughing so hard she could not say anything.

"Who is she? And why is she laughing at me?" asked Danny.

"I am Millicent the acrobat and I think you are funny."

Danny looked so sad and pitiful that Millicent felt badly. She had hurt Danny's feelings by laughing at him. She had an idea, "So Danny, how did you learn to do a double-back summersault? That was really good, I am a trained acrobat and I can only do one summersault at a time."

Danny's chest puffed up and he said proudly, "I guess it just comes naturally to a hedgehog, some things I just know how to do!"

Laurel knew at that moment that she and Millicent would be new best friends. Even though Millicent did not know Danny, she had noticed that he was sad and she made him feel better by making a bad situation seem like a good one.

Danny started telling Millicent stories of some of the other talents that he had and things that he had seen. Millicent listened very carefully and agreed with Danny several times. They all had a good time just getting to know one another.

The afternoon was almost over and Laurel was sad to think of Millicent going back to her home. Laurel asked, "Millicent, would you like to stay with me in my treehouse? I can introduce you to all of my friends in Periwinkle Woods and you will never have to go across the big scary road again."

Millicent replied, "I would be very happy to stay in such a beautiful place! Would you call me Millie? All my good friends call me Millie." Laurel showed Millie the way back to her tree house and they talked most of the night about the many important things in the life of girl squirrels.

Late that night as Laurel curled up in her bed she thought about the day. She realized that today had been a very special day indeed and she could hardly wait to find what tomorrow would bring.

THE END

Laurel Finds A Friend

Amazon, Books A Million and Barnes & Nobel
Reviews are appreciated